Drew
the Screw

Drew the Screw

MATTIA CERATO

I Like to Read®

Holiday House / New York

To Vale, my family and all the people
who always supported me

Copyright © 2016 by Mattia Cerato
All Rights Reserved
HOLIDAY HOUSE is registered in the U.S. Patent and Trademark Office.
Printed and Bound in November 2015 at Tien Wah Press, Johor Bahru, Johor, Malaysia.
The artwork was created with digital tools.
www.holidayhouse.com
First Edition
1 3 5 7 9 10 8 6 4 2

Library of Congress Cataloging-in-Publication Data
Cerato, Mattia, author, illustrator.
Drew the screw / Mattia Cerato. — First edition.
pages cm. — (I like to read)
Summary: The saw cuts, the hammer hits, and the drill
makes holes; so Drew needs a job too.
ISBN 978-0-8234-3540-1 (hardcover)
[1. Screws—Fiction. 2. Tools—Fiction.] I. Title.
PZ7.C3186Dr 2016
[E]—dc23
2015015546

ISBN 978-0-8234-3541-8 (paperback)

I am Drew the screw.

I live here.

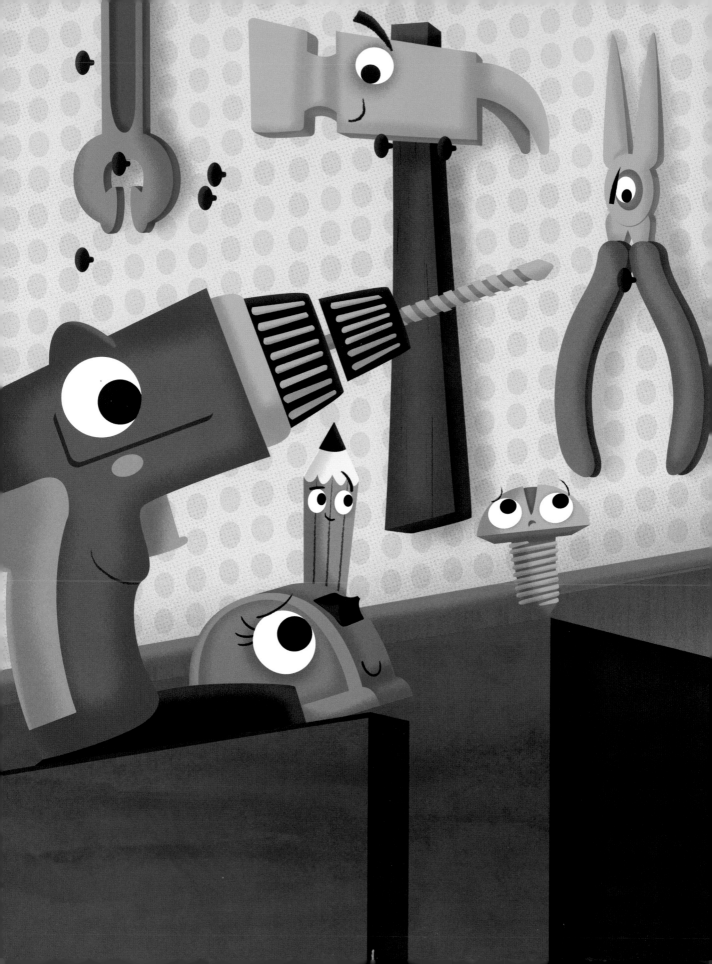

I hang out with the tools.

The pencil makes lines.

The tape measures.

The saw cuts.

The hammer hits.

The clamp
holds things.

The drill makes holes.

The tools ask,
"What can you do?"

The boy has come for me.

We go up.

Now I have a job
to do too.

You will like these too!

Come Back, Ben by Ann Hassett and John Hassett
A *Kirkus Reviews* Best Book

Dinosaurs Don't, Dinosaurs Do by Steve Björkman
A Notable Social Studies Trade Book for Young People
An IRA/CBC Children's Choice

Fish Had a Wish by Michael Garland
A *Kirkus Reviews* Best Book
A Top 25 Children's Books list book

The Fly Flew In by David Catrow
An IRA/CBC Children's Choice
Maryland Blue Crab Young Reader Award Winner

Look! by Ted Lewin
The Correll Book Award for Excellence
in Early Childhood Informational Text

Me Too! by Valeri Gorbachev
A Bank Street Best Children's Book of the Year

Mice on Ice by Rebecca Emberley and Ed Emberley
A Bank Street Best Children's Book of the Year
An IRA/CBC Children's Choice

Pig Has a Plan by Ethan Long
An IRA/CBC Children's Choice

See Me Dig by Paul Meisel
A *Kirkus Reviews* Best Book

See Me Run by Paul Meisel
A Theodor Seuss Geisel Award Honor Book
An ALA Notable Children's Book

You Can Do It! by Betsy Lewin
A Bank Street Best Children's Book of the Year,
Outstanding Merit

See more I Like to Read® books.
Go to www.holidayhouse.com/I-Like-to-Read/

Some More I Like to Read® Books in Paperback

Animals Work by Ted Lewin

Bad Dog by David McPhail

Big Cat by Ethan Long

Can You See Me? by Ted Lewin

Cat Got a Lot by Steve Henry

Drew the Screw by Mattia Cerato

The Fly Flew In by David Catrow

Happy Cat by Steve Henry

Here Is Big Bunny by Steve Henry

I Have a Garden by Bob Barner

I See and See by Ted Lewin

Little Ducks Go by Emily Arnold McCully

Me Too! by Valeri Gorbachev

Mice on Ice by Rebecca Emberley and Ed Emberley

Not Me! by Valeri Gorbachev

Pig Has a Plan by Ethan Long

Pig Is Big on Books by Douglas Florian

What Am I? Where Am I? by Ted Lewin

You Can Do It! by Betsy Lewin

Visit http://www.holidayhouse.com/I-Like-to-Read/ for more about I Like to Read® books,
including flash cards, reproducibles and the complete list of titles.